D0500695

RECEIVED

OCT 1 5 2018

Douglass-Truth Branch Library

NO LONGER PROPERTY OF
SEATTLE PUBLIC LIBRARY

Josie's Lost Tooth

Jennifer K. Mann

CANDLEWICK PRESS

Josie was the monkey-bars champion of her class.

She was the first one to
read a whole book by herself,

and she was *almost* the
fastest runner at recess.

But Josie was the *only* one in her class who hadn't lost a tooth.

Not a single one.

Mrs. Geldart's Class
Blueberry Hill Elementary

When Richard lost his first tooth, he showed Josie the coin he got from the Tooth Fairy.

"She sneaks into your room when you're asleep and takes your tooth?" Josie asked.

"Yup," said Richard. "And she gives you money for it."

Josie checked for a loose tooth every night.

But nothing ever moved, not even a bit.

"I lost a tooth at breakfast," Richard said one morning. "I brought it in with my shark tooth for show-and-tell. Sharks' teeth fall out when they chomp into boats and giant squids."

"I wish I could chomp into a squid," said Josie.

That night when Josie checked her teeth, she felt one move, just a little. Finally — a loose tooth!

She couldn't wait to show Richard.

"Look!" said Josie at school the next morning. "I have a loose tooth! I'm going to hang upside down until it falls out!"

"Cool," said Richard. "Can I have a turn when you're done?"

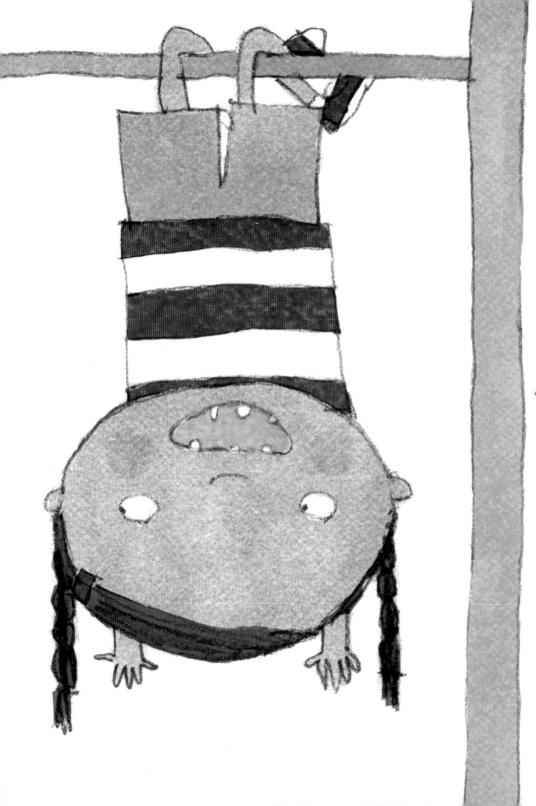

But when the bell rang a few minutes later, Josie's tooth was still attached.

At lunch, Josie saved her apple for last.

"My tooth is going to come out when I chomp into this apple — like when a shark chomps on a squid," she said.

CHOMP!

"Your tooth is still there, Josie," said Richard. "Want to try my carrot sticks instead?" But those didn't work, either.

When Josie found Richard at recess, she said, "Watch this! I'm going to pull my tooth out with a string."

"Did it work?" she asked.

Richard looked inside Josie's mouth.

"Still there," he said.

Josie wondered if she would ever get a coin from the Tooth Fairy.
What if she had baby teeth for the rest of her life?

Just then, Richard ran by. "Want to play sharks?" he asked.

"All right," said Josie. "I'll be the shark!"

But just when Josie was about to catch up with Richard . . .

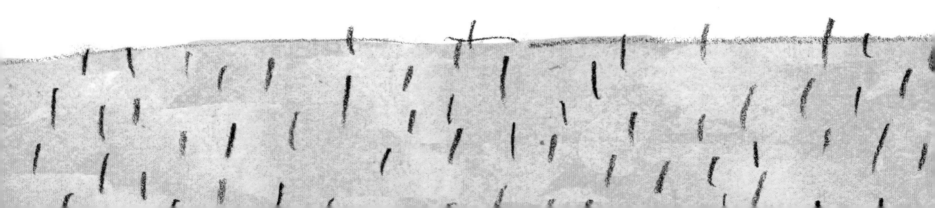

she tripped.

SPLAT!

Josie felt around in her mouth with her tongue — her tooth was gone!

"Oh, no!" she gasped. "My tooth!"

Richard helped her look for it, but Josie's tooth was nowhere to be found.

"Maybe you swallowed it," he said.

While Josie was in the nurse's office, Richard tried to cheer her up.

"At least you finally lost a tooth!" he said.

"I didn't want to *lose* it, though," said Josie. "Now what will I leave for the Tooth Fairy?"

"You can try leaving my shark tooth," Richard offered.

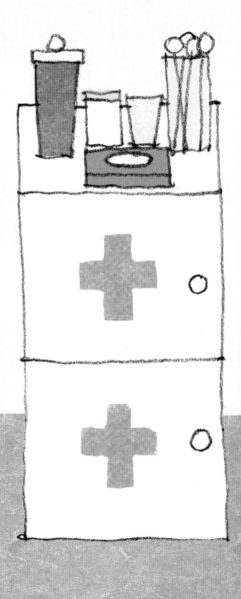

That night, Josie held the shark tooth up to her gap.

It made her look pretty sharky, but it wasn't her own tooth.

She decided to leave a note for the Tooth Fairy under her pillow with the shark tooth.

Dear Tooth Fairy,
I lost a tooth today, but I can't find it. My friend Richard said I could leave his shark tooth for you instead. I'm the last one in my class to lose a tooth, so please still leave me a coin.

Love,
Josie

When Josie checked under her pillow in the morning, there was a note from the Tooth Fairy — and something else.
She couldn't wait to show Richard.

"You got a shark tooth necklace?" asked Richard.

"Yup," said Josie. "And she left one for you, too!"

"Cool," said Richard. "Want to play sharks?"

"OK," said Josie. "You can be the shark and I'll be the squid."

Dear Josie,

I know that you did lose a tooth, and I am sorry that it got lost.

Here is a shark tooth necklace for you — and one for your friend Richard, too.

Love,
The Tooth Fairy

For E + N, who inspire me daily

Copyright © 2018 by Jennifer K. Mann

All rights reserved. No part of this book may be reproduced, transmitted, or stored in an information retrieval system in any form or by any means, graphic, electronic, or mechanical, including photocopying, taping, and recording, without prior written permission from the publisher.

First edition 2018

Library of Congress Catalog Card Number pending
ISBN 978-0-7636-9694-8

LEO 23 22 21 20 19 18
10 9 8 7 6 5 4 3 2 1

Printed in Heshan, Guangdong, China

This book was typeset in Kosmik.
The illustrations were done in pencil and pastel and combined digitally.

Candlewick Press
99 Dover Street
Somerville, Massachusetts 02144

visit us at www.candlewick.com